One coincidence too many?

FRANKENSTEIN	MR. FRANK
pale and thin	pale and thin
workshop filthy	very messy
experimented with electricity	uses a lot of electricity
nobody liked him	nobody likes him

FRANKENSTEIN

Moved in on the Fourth Floor

ALSO BY ELIZABETH LEVY
Published by HarperCollins Publishers

Dracula Is a Pain in the Neck

Gorgonzola Zombies in the Park

Keep Ms. Sugarman in the Fourth Grade

School Spirit Sabotage
A Brian and Pea Brain Mystery

Rude Rowdy Rumors
A Brian and Pea Brain Mystery

FRANKENSTEIN
Moved in on the Fourth Floor

by Elizabeth Levy

illustrated by
Mordicai Gerstein

HarperTrophy
A Division of HarperCollinsPublishers

Library of Congress Cataloging-in-Publication Data
Levy, Elizabeth
  Frankenstein moved in on the fourth floor / Levy, Elizabeth

    Summary: Robert and Sam suspect their weird new neighbor is really Franken-
stein.
    [1. Apartment houses—Fiction.]   I. Gerstein, Mordicai.   II. Title.
PZ7.L5827Fr   1979   [Fic]   78-19830
ISBN 0-06-023810-0
ISBN 0-06-023811-9 (lib. bdg.)
ISBN 0-06-440122-7 (pbk.)

First Harper Trophy edition, 1981.

To David and Ben

CONTENTS

FRANKENSTEIN

Moved in on the
Fourth Floor

1

In the Stairwell

Sam pushed the button for the elevator, but it didn't come. He and his mother waited and waited. They were going to pick up Sam's younger brother, Robert, who was playing at a friend's house.

"Maybe the elevator's broken," said Sam.

"It seems to be stuck on the fourth floor," said Mrs. Bamford, looking at the numbers above the elevator. She pushed the button again, but the elevator didn't move. After another few minutes, Mrs. Bamford sighed. They lived on the nineteenth floor.

"I guess we'll have to use the stairs," she said. Sam ran down the stairs holding on to the railing. Mrs. Bamford walked more slowly, shouting, "Don't get too far ahead," but Sam was already far ahead of her.

When he got to the fourth floor, Sam saw a pile of boxes on the landing, each filled with bits of different colored wires. Sam pulled out a tangled mess of wire. Suddenly the stairwell door opened and a very strange head with earphones and antennas poked out.

"Leave that stuff alone," the head shouted.

"Ohh!" yelled Sam, so surprised that he jumped back.

"Sam? Are you all right?" shouted Mrs. Bamford, still two stories above.

The head disappeared back into the hallway.

"What happened?" shouted Mrs. Bamford as she ran down the stairs to Sam.

"A monster just shouted at me," said Sam.

"A monster?" Mrs. Bamford looked around at all the boxes. "What is all this?" she asked.

"It belongs to the monster," said Sam. "He looked like a martian."

Mrs. Bamford noticed they were on the fourth floor. "Let's see why the elevator's stuck here," she said, opening the door.

The fourth floor hallway was a mess with boxes all over. Each one had "Frank" written on it. Some boxes propped the elevator doors open, and a trail of boxes led to apartment 4E.

In the middle of the living room of 4E, the man with the earphones and antennas on his head sat cross-legged on the floor, surrounded by wires.

"Excuse me, are those your boxes in the hall?" asked Mrs. Bamford. The man ignored her. Mrs. Bamford asked again. Finally she walked over and tapped him on the shoulder.

"What do you want?" growled the man, taking off his earphones and laying them on the floor.

"Is your name Frank?" asked Mrs. Bamford.

"Yeah, I'm Mr. Frank. I just moved in."

"Your boxes are holding up the elevator," said Mrs. Bamford. "We just walked down fifteen stories."

"I have very delicate equipment in those boxes. I have to move them slowly," said Mr. Frank.

While they were talking, Sam inched closer to the earphones to inspect them. He could hear strange music playing softly. Gingerly, Sam picked up the earphones to hear the music better, and just to see what they felt like he slipped them over his ears.

Suddenly they were plucked off his head by Mr. Frank, who shouted, "Those are mine!"

"Mr. Frank!" said Mrs. Bamford. "You didn't have to grab. Sam would have given them back to you if you had asked."

Mr. Frank didn't hear her because he had his earphones back on.

Mrs. Bamford took Sam's hand and marched to the elevator. She shoved Mr. Frank's boxes away from the elevator doors and pushed the button for down.

"I've never met anybody so rude in my whole life," said Mrs. Bamford as the doors closed. "You were right. He is a monster."

When they got to the first floor, five people were waiting for the elevator.

"We thought it was broken," said Ms. Anderson, who lived in 11A.

"We've been waiting fifteen minutes," said Mr. Ferguson in 5F. "Have you had it tied up all this time?"

"No," said Mrs. Bamford. "Someone on the fourth floor is moving in."

"That *must* be Mr. Frank," said Mr. Clem from 4F. "He's been moving in boxes since early this morning. I hate to make a snap judgment about a new neighbor, but he was very rude to me today."

"He was rude to me too," said Mrs. Bamford.

"I offered to help him," said Mr. Clem. "But he didn't want anybody touching his boxes. . . . I don't know. There was something about him I didn't like."

"Oh, Mr. Clem," said Ms. Anderson. "You always look on the gloomy side. He could turn out to be a fine neighbor."

"I have my doubts," said Mrs. Bamford.

The other tenants got into the elevator, and Sam and his mother went to get Robert at his friend's house. As they were walking home Robert said, "Look what Jimmy gave me." He held out a Dracula doll.

"One of its fangs is broken," said Sam.

"I don't care," said Robert.

"What did you trade him for it?" asked Sam.

"A Frankenstein," said Robert. "But I had two anyhow."

"I hope you didn't trade him *my* Frankenstein."

"No, it was mine," said Robert. "It had the red shirt on."

As they got into the elevator, Sam said, "I hope the elevator doesn't stop at four. Right, Mom?"

"Why?" asked Robert.

"A Mr. Frank moved in. He is weird."

Robert wrapped the cloak around his new Dracula doll. "Dracula's neat," he said.

"Mr. Frank acted really, really weird," said Sam. "He and Mom had a fight."

Robert kept playing with his Dracula doll. They got out on the nineteenth floor and went into their apartment.

"He could be the real Frankenstein . . ." Sam whispered into Robert's ear. "He had wires sticking up all over his head."

They went into their room to play before dinner.

"If Frankenstein moved in, Mom would have told me," said Robert.

"She didn't want to scare you. You're too little."

Later that night when they were getting ready for bed, Robert said, "You were kidding, weren't you? Frankenstein didn't move in on the fourth floor."

"No, I wasn't kidding."

"Frankenstein wouldn't fit in the elevator," Robert protested. "He's about ten feet tall."

"Frankenstein isn't the monster," explained Sam. "He's the man who made the monster. Remember, we saw the movie."

"I remember," said Robert, but the truth was he couldn't remember it too well.

"You're just trying to scare me," said Robert.

"No I'm not."

"Want to play with my Dracula doll?" asked Robert.

"No, I want to look at my Frankenstein book. There's something I want to check."

Sam went to his bed table and pulled out the biggest book.

FRANKENSTEIN
by Mary Shelley (abridged version)

Robert looked over his shoulder. "Read it to me."

"It's a very hard book," said Sam. "It was written a long time ago."

"I know," said Robert. "Just read the good parts."

"... *It was a dreary night of November. . . . Working alone in my workshop of filthy creation . . . my cheek had grown pale . . . my person had become emaciated. . . .*"

"Mr. Frank is very thin," said Sam. "That's one of the things I wanted to check out."

Robert didn't say anything.

"Who shall conceive the horrors of my secret toil, as I dabbled among the unhallowed damps of the grave . . . ?"

"Does that mean he went around stealing bodies from graveyards?" asked Robert.

"He needed bits and pieces of bodies to make his monster," Sam said.

". . . I saw the dull yellow eye of my creature open; it breathed hard. . . . His yellow skin scarcely covered the work of muscles. . . . His jaws opened. . . ."

"Did he have fangs?" asked Robert.

"No, that's Dracula."

"That's not the end, is it?" asked Robert.

"No. It gets a lot scarier."

"Yeah," said Robert. "But it's just a story. . . . Go on."

Sam finished reading.

The next day Robert and Sam went down to the basement.

"Do you want to find Frankenstein's storage room?" Sam asked.

"You're just making all this up," said Robert.

"I'm not," said Sam. "I'll show you." He started down the hall. Robert didn't want to go with him, but he didn't want to be left alone in the basement either.

They walked down the corridor. This part of the basement had only a few bare light bulbs hanging from the ceiling. Each tenant had a little room with his or her name on the door. Every once in a while there was a place where a bulb had burned out, and it was very dark in the narrow passageway between the storage rooms.

Sam pointed to a room with a new sign on it. "What does it say?" asked Robert.

"Frank," said Sam. "See, it starts with F."

"It says Frank. It doesn't say Frankenstein," said Robert, staring at the sign.

"Frank could be short for Frankenstein," said Sam. "He wouldn't dare give his whole name because no one would let Frankenstein live in our building."

"What do you think's in there?" asked Robert.

"Maybe he keeps all his dead bodies in there," said Sam.

"How many dead bodies do you think he's got?" asked Robert.

"Trillions!" said Sam.

"He couldn't keep trillions in there," said Robert. "They wouldn't fit and they'd smell."

Sam and Robert pushed their noses to the keyhole. It smelled musty.

"I think we should go back," said Robert.

"Me too," said Sam.

2

Blackout

About a week later Robert and Sam were playing in the swings outside their apartment building. It was very windy. A gust of wind sent a pile of cardboard boxes flying, bouncing in front of the building. Mr. Christiansen, the super, ran after them, but the wind blew them in all directions.

Sam and Robert jumped off the swings to help. The boxes were big and clumsy, and every time Sam or Robert grabbed one, another would fly away from them. One of the boxes flew up and hit Mr. Christiansen in the nose, knocking off his glasses.

"Ohh," shouted Mr. Christiansen. "If I get

my hands on that man . . ."

"What man?" shouted Sam, wrestling a box to the ground, and getting it under a rock.

"That Mr. Frank," shouted Mr. Christiansen. Robert found Mr. Christiansen's glasses and handed them to him.

"All these boxes are his," said Mr. Christiansen. "I don't know what he keeps in them, but he keeps bringing more and more into his apartment, and then he never ties the empty ones together like I ask him. It's a disgrace."

Mr. Christiansen bent over to pick up the last boxes.

"What's this!" he cried, picking up Robert's Dracula doll.

"It's mine, Mr. Christiansen . . ." said Robert. "I dropped it."

"Yours?"

"Yes, it's my Dracula doll . . . see it's got a fang missing?"

"Oh," said Mr. Christiansen. "Well, here you are Robert. You and your brother are good kids, not like some people around here."

Sam and Robert heard nothing more about Mr. Frank for quite a few days. Then one afternoon they were in the supermarket with their mother, and they saw Mr. Clem picking out a head of cabbage.

"Hello, Mr. Clem. How are you?" said Mrs. Bamford.

Mr. Clem ignored her.

"That's strange," said Mrs. Bamford. "Mr. Clem is always friendly—gloomy, but friendly."

Sam and Robert pushed the cart around the aisles. As they turned the corner by the breakfast cereals, they almost ran into Mr. Clem.

"Hello, Sam and Robert . . . Mrs. Bamford," said Mr. Clem cheerily.

"Hello!" said Mrs. Bamford. "We saw you before, but I guess you didn't hear us."

"What?" exclaimed Mr. Clem loudly.

"I SAID WE SAID HELLO BEFORE," shouted Mrs. Bamford.

"Oh, wait a minute," said Mr. Clem. "I have my earplugs in." He pulled out a pair of earplugs from his ears. "I'm sorry, I forgot I had these in," said Mr. Clem.

"Excuse me for asking," said Mrs. Bamford, "but why do you wear earplugs in the supermarket? Does the piped-in music bother you?"

"No . . . Muzak is a choir of angels compared to what I have to listen to. It's that Mr. Frank. He isn't fit to be a neighbor."

"What do you mean?" asked Mrs. Bamford.

Sam and Robert exchanged looks.

"I keep hearing the strangest sounds from his apartment . . . moans and groans. He tells me it's his music. If that's music my name is Mozart. That's why I got the earplugs," said Mr. Clem.

"I have to admit I did not enjoy my little run-in with him," said Mrs. Bamford. "He is a very annoying man."

"Annoying is mild for what I'd call him," said Mr. Clem.

Robert and Sam looked at each other. Mrs. Bamford finished her grocery shopping and they walked back home. "It's late," said Mrs. Bamford. "It's almost dark."

When they got in front of their building, the light over the front door was out.

"It must have burned out," said Mrs. Bamford.

"I'll have to tell Mr. Christiansen." But when they opened the front door, they were in for a surprise. The lobby was dark also.

"What's going on?" exclaimed Mrs. Bamford.

"Maybe it's a blackout," said Robert.

"No," said Sam. "The streetlights are on."

"Who's there?" said a voice.

"It's the Bamfords," said Mrs. Bamford.

"It's Mr. Christiansen. . . . The lights are out in the whole building. I have candles."

Soon the lobby was filled with flickering lights.

"How did it happen?" asked Mrs. Bamford.

"It started on the fourth floor," said Mr. Christiansen. "Somebody up there must have overloaded the circuits."

"Ha!" said Mr. Clem, who had just come back from the supermarket. "I know who's to blame."

"Will it be fixed soon?" asked Mrs. Bamford.

"I'm waiting for the electrician," said Mr. Christiansen with a sigh. "He said he'll be here as soon as he can."

"But we have to go to the nineteenth floor," said Mrs. Bamford.

"I can give you candles," said Mr. Christiansen.

"Sam and Robert, it looks like we're going to

get some exercise," said Mrs. Bamford. "Leave the groceries down here. We have enough food up in the apartment."

Mrs. Bamford took a lighted candle from Mr. Christiansen, and they started up the stairwell. It was very dark.

"Hold on to my hand, Robert," said Mrs. Bamford. "Sam, you hold on to Robert."

"Our voices sound all funny," said Sam.

"That's because of the echo in the stairwell," said Mrs. Bamford. "There's nothing to be frightened of."

"I don't understand," said Robert. "Why did all the lights go off?"

"Frankenstein did it . . ." whispered Sam.

"Sam, stop trying to scare your brother. Maybe we should sing." Mrs. Bamford began to sing, "We are climbing Jacob's ladder . . ."

Sam and Robert chimed in, but they kept singing it slower and slower. "It sounds like a funeral march," said Mrs. Bamford. "Let's sing something else."

Sam started to sing, "We all live in a yellow submarine . . ." and they picked up the pace.

"What floor are we on?" asked Sam.

Just then they felt a slight breeze and Mrs. Bamford's candle blew out. The stairwell became as black as ink—not even a sliver of light.

"Don't panic . . . don't panic," said Mrs. Bamford, but her voice sounded very anxious. She got a match and relit her candle.

"Who's there?" she shouted.

"It's Mr. Frank!" shouted a very gruff voice. Robert and Sam grabbed each other's hand.

"When are the lights going back on?" shouted Mr. Frank. "I was working on something new and suddenly the lights went out. This could ruin my equipment."

"The lights are off in the whole building," said Mrs. Bamford. "It started on the fourth floor."

"I don't know if I like living in a place that always has blackouts," muttered Mr. Frank.

"We didn't have them until you moved in," said Mrs. Bamford.

"Mom," whispered Sam, "don't get into a fight with him in the dark."

"The people in this building are just too nosy," said Mr. Frank. He slammed the door on the stairwell and the breeze from the door blew out Mrs. Bamford's candle once again.

"That man *is* a monster!" said Mrs. Bamford, very annoyed. She relit her candle.

"Come on, boys, we still have fifteen floors to go. We need a long song. How about 'One Hundred Bottles of Beer on the Wall'?"

"I hate that song," said Sam.

"Me too," said Mrs. Bamford, "but it's the longest one I know."

They were singing, "Six bottles of beer on the wall . . . six bottles of beer . . ." when they got to the nineteenth floor. Mrs. Bamford lit lots of candles around the living room, and soon it looked like a party.

Robert kept singing, "Four bottles of beer on the wall . . ."

"I don't want to ever sing that song again," said Mrs. Bamford, collapsing on the couch.

"But we've never come so close to finishing."

"Oh all right," said Mrs. Bamford. By the time they got to "ONE BOTTLE OF BEER ON THE WALL" they were all singing at the top of their lungs.

"That's it," said Mrs. Bamford when they finished. "If either of you kids ever sings that song again I'll . . ." Suddenly the lights in the apartment went on.

"Hooray!" shouted Sam and Robert.

"What about the groceries we left downstairs?" asked Robert.

"Oh . . . I forgot all about them," said Mrs. Bamford.

"The elevator must be working," said Sam, "now that the electricity's back on. We'll go get the food, Mom."

When Sam and Robert got down to the lobby they found Mr. Christiansen talking to the electrician.

"It definitely started in 4E," said the electrician.

"That's Mr. Frank's apartment," said Mr. Christiansen. "I might have known."

"He must have been using an awful lot of electricity for something," said the electrician. "It's very unusual to overload a whole building."

"He's a strange tenant," said Mr. Christiansen. "He's got all this electronic equipment. I don't know what he does with it."

Sam and Robert picked up the groceries and got back on the elevator. Sam was very thoughtful. He watched the lights above the door.

"Robert . . ." he said finally. "Suppose Mr. Frank really is Frankenstein . . ."

"Huh!" said Robert, who was poking in the grocery bag to see if Mom had bought chocolate chip cookies.

"I'm serious," said Sam. "You heard the electrician. Mr. Frank was using an awful lot of electricity."

"So what?" said Robert. "Look . . . Mom got two kinds of cookies."

"Robert! This is much more important than cookies. Frankenstein made the monster out of electricity. He could be making another monster right in our building."

When they got back to the apartment, Sam got out his Frankenstein book and turned to the page showing Dr. Frankenstein making the monster. The room was full of bizarre-looking electrical equipment. Sam started to leaf through the book. Then he got a pencil and paper.

"What are you doing?" asked Robert.

"I'm making a list," said Sam.

FRANKENSTEIN	MR. FRANK
pale and thin	pale and thin
workshop filthy	very messy (according to Mr. Christiansen)
experiments with electricity	uses a lot of electricity
moans and groans from the floor where he worked	moans and groans on the fourth floor (according to Mr. Clem)
nobody liked him once he started to make the monster	nobody likes him —Mr. Christiansen —Mr. Clem —Mom

"I think there are just too many coincidences," said Sam after he finished. He showed Robert the list.

"Sam, you really think he's Frankenstein?" asked Robert.

"I think so," said Sam slowly. "Frankenstein moved in and nobody knows it but us. . . ." Sam's voice was barely above a whisper.

"Maybe we should tell Mom about it," said Robert.

"No . . ." said Sam. "Not yet . . . we need proof. She'll think we're only fooling. Nobody's going to believe he's the real Frankenstein unless we get evidence. . . ."

"Yeah, but if he's the real Frankenstein . . . we could get . . ." Robert's voice trailed off.

"I know . . ." said Sam.

They both were quiet for a moment. "I think it will be too dangerous to try to get into his apartment," said Sam.

"Yeah," said Robert. "Way too dangerous."

"But," said Sam, "we could try to find out what he's got hidden in his storage room."

"I don't know . . ." said Robert.

"Listen . . . we've got a right to be in the basement . . . we have a storage room down there, too. I bet he hardly ever goes down there, and if we can just get into his room . . . he might have old monster-making equipment stored there. *Then* we could go to Mom, and she'd believe us, and she could call the cops."

"But what if he catches us," said Robert.

"He won't," said Sam. "We'll be very, very careful."

3

In Frankenstein's
Storage Room

The next morning Sam told his mother they were going downstairs to play. Robert had his Dracula doll in his hand.

"Fine," said Mrs. Bamford. "Just be sure to stay near the building. Play in our playground."

While they were waiting for the elevator Robert said, "You shouldn't have lied to Mom."

"I didn't," said Sam. "I said we were going downstairs and we are."

"But maybe we should just go out to the playground and go to Frankenstein's storage room some other time."

"No," said Sam. "This is something we've got to do." Sam suddenly pushed the button for four.

"What did you do that for?" shouted Robert.

"Shhh," said Sam. "We have to stop on the fourth floor to try to find out if he's in his apartment. If he is, then we'll know it'll be safe to go to the basement."

"What if he's in the hallway and catches us?" asked Robert.

Before Sam could answer, the door opened onto the fourth floor.

Sam peered out.

The hallway was empty.

"I'm staying in the elevator," said Robert. "You go ring his doorbell."

"Come on," said Sam. "We'll just eavesdrop."

"I don't want to eavesdrop on Frankenstein," said Robert.

"Would you rather he caught us in the basement?" said Sam. "I'll go alone."

Robert stayed in the elevator. Sam walked as silently as he could to 4E. He could hear loud, peculiar music coming from inside.

Robert hopped from foot to foot in the elevator. Then before he could stop them, the elevator doors started to close. Sam ran back to the

elevator, but the elevator was gone before he got there. Without thinking, Sam pounded on the elevator door.

He heard a door open behind him.

He whirled around. It was Mr. Clem.

"What are you doing?" asked Mr. Clem.

"Uhh . . . nothing . . ." said Sam.

"What?" shouted Mr. Clem. "Oh, my earplugs . . ." Mr. Clem took out his earplugs. "He's making that music again," explained Mr. Clem.

"I heard," whispered Sam.

"You don't have to whisper," said Mr. Clem. "He can't hear anything with that music going on. Sometimes I think I should call the cops. I've already called the landlord."

"What do you think he's doing in there?" whispered Sam.

"I don't know," said Mr. Clem. "What did you say you were doing on the fourth floor?"

"Nothing," said Sam. "I got out on the wrong floor."

"How strange," said Mr. Clem. "Four is nowhere near nineteen. This building is getting most peculiar."

The elevator opened and Robert was inside, looking very scared. Sam got in. "You left me all alone," he said angrily.

"I did not," said Robert. "The doors just closed. Somebody needed the elevator."

"Frankenstein could have grabbed me," said Sam.

"Did he find you?" asked Robert in a whisper.

"No . . ." said Sam. "I was lucky. Anyhow he's in there all right . . . making weird noises. He might have his new monster finished any day now."

When they got to the basement they walked straight to Frankenstein's storage room. There was a huge lock on the door.

"That lock wasn't there before," whispered Robert.

"It's the biggest lock in the place," said Sam shaking the chain. "He really must have something to hide."

"We'll never get in," said Robert. "We'd better go back."

"No," said Sam. "Wait a minute." Sam looked around. The partitions for the storage rooms were built only halfway up with plywood, and then chicken wire went up to the ceiling. Sam got a bunch of boxes from the corner and piled them next to the partition.

"Please," said Robert. "Let's go back."

"Robert . . . this is important. We've got to

find out what's in there." Sam climbed onto the boxes.

"I don't think we should spy on Frankenstein without a grown-up," insisted Robert.

"We've got to prove he *is* Frankenstein," said Sam. "We can't go back yet." Sam peered through the chicken wire. "I can't see anything. . . . It's too dark." Sam started to poke at the chicken wire. There was a small space where a nail was missing. Sam looked down at Robert. "I think there's a hole here where you could get in."

"I'm not going in there," said Robert.

"It isn't big enough for me," said Sam. "I'll help you through."

"No!"

"Look, he's upstairs. He isn't going to catch you. Besides, you left me all alone on the fourth floor."

"I did not."

"You did too!"

"I didn't mean to!"

"Come on, Robert, you have to do this. Then we'll find out once and for all if he is Frankenstein."

Robert climbed up onto the boxes next to Sam.

"I don't think I can get through," he said.

"Try," said Sam. He helped Robert squirm through the hole in the chicken wire.

Robert dropped down to the floor. It was dark in the storage room. He felt boxes all around him.

"Can you see anything?" Sam asked.

"No," said Robert.

"Find the light switch. It's probably in the middle of the room, on a chain."

"I can see it . . . it's just that there's all this stuff in the way. It's very creepy in here."

"You're doing great, Robert," said Sam.

Robert felt his way over to the light chain and pulled it.

When the light went on both Robert and Sam gasped.

The room was piled to the ceiling with broken record players, radios, and wires everywhere, wires of every different color and thickness.

"Look at all this stuff," whispered Sam, peering through the chicken wire.

"I'm getting out of here," said Robert.

"Wait a second," said Sam. "We need to see if he's got any equipment just like in the book."

"I'm scared, Sam."

"It does look like Frankenstein's workshop, all right," whispered Sam.

"I'm not staying in here," said Robert. He started to climb out. He was almost all the way to the top when his foot hit a box and it crashed to the floor. Hundreds of tiny glass electronic tubes chattered to the floor.

Sam pulled Robert the rest of the way through the hole.

"You're not hurt, are you?" asked Sam anxiously. "Did you get cut?"

"No," said Robert, but he was shaking. He stared at the broken glass on the floor. "What are we going to do?" he sobbed.

"Let's get out of here," said Sam. They ran back to the elevator.

"We're going to get in trouble," whispered Robert.

"Maybe he won't know we did it," said Sam.

"But we broke all that glass," said Robert.

"Yeah, I know," said Sam, "but if we don't tell, maybe he'll think a cat did it."

"I think we should tell Mom," said Robert.

"Let's wait and see what happens, and then figure out what to do," said Sam.

At dinner that night Mrs. Bamford asked, "Is something wrong?"

"No," said Sam in a very quiet voice.

Robert didn't say anything.

"It's not like both of you to be so quiet," said

Mrs. Bamford. "Do you feel okay?"

"Mom," said Robert. "Do you know Frankenstein?"

"Of course," said Mrs. Bamford. "What about Frankenstein?"

"What do you know about him?" asked Robert.

"He made a monster out of bits and pieces of old wire and electricity. Why are you interested?"

Robert didn't answer. He didn't even want dessert.

4

The Chase

The next morning Robert woke up with a terrible feeling in the pit of his stomach. It was very early. He went over to Sam's bed and shook him awake.

"Sam . . ."

"What?" asked Sam, still half asleep.

"Sam, wake up!"

"What do you want, Robert?"

"Are you awake?"

"I am now."

"I've got something awful to tell you."

"What?"

"I lost my Dracula doll."

"You woke me up to tell me that . . . ?"

"No . . . it's worse."

"What's worse?"

"Frankenstein's got Dracula!"

"Huh!"

"FRANKENSTEIN HAS GOT DRACULA!" repeated Robert. "I left my Dracula in Frankenstein's storage room and we left the light on. He's going to know it was us."

Sam just stared at Robert.

"Are you sure?" he asked finally.

Robert nodded his head. "I had it in my hand when I was climbing out and I must have dropped it when I kicked the box."

"That was real stupid."

"It was your stupid idea to go in there."

"Maybe he won't know it belongs to you."

"How many other kids around here have a Dracula with one fang?" said Robert. "Lots of people have seen me with it. Mr. Christiansen knows it's mine. Remember when he looked at it in the playground."

"I forgot," said Sam.

"Yeah," said Robert.

"I'll bet if Frankenstein finds it, the first person he'll go to is Mr. Christiansen."

Robert looked scared.

"Frankenstein's going to hate me."

"Wait a minute, Robert. Maybe we can

sneak back down there and get Dracula and clean up the mess before he finds it."

"What if he's there?"

"It's six-thirty in the morning. What would he be doing down there this early?"

"He could be making another monster," Robert suggested.

"We should at least go look," said Sam. "We could clean it up and nobody would know we were even there."

Sam and Robert tiptoed out into the hall and rang for the elevator. Sam pushed the button for the basement. It was as quiet as a graveyard down in the basement.

"I don't think anybody's down here," whispered Sam.

But when they got to Mr. Frank's storage room, they were surprised. A sign "KEEP OUT! PRIVATE!" was nailed across the spot where Robert had crawled through the chicken wire, and the light in the storage room was out.

"Oh, NO!" cried Robert.

Sam stared at the sign. "Frankenstein found the broken glass," he said quietly.

"And my Dracula . . ." said Robert. "I have a stomachache."

"Yeah, if he found the Dracula . . . he'll find out it was you."

"ME! I would never have gone in there if you hadn't made me."

"I meant us. I'm sorry."

"I hate it down here. Let's go. . . ."

"Just a second . . . suppose he didn't find your Dracula."

"I'm going."

Sam started to climb up on the pile of boxes next to the storage room.

"I'm not staying here," said Robert.

Robert started to walk away, but Sam didn't notice. Sam was trying to peer through the darkness. Suddenly Sam's head bumped against a small black box firmly secured to the chicken wire.

"Hey what's this . . . it wasn't here yesterday . . ."

Sam looked down. "Robert . . . Robert? . . ."

Sam looked all round.

He began to get scared.

Suddenly he heard the elevator door open in the basement. And then he heard a voice shout, "You must be the kid I'm looking for."

Robert screamed.

"Hey!" said the voice. "Hold still!"

"Sam!" yelled Robert. "Frankenstein's got me!"

Sam ran through the maze of storage bins. When he got to the elevator he saw Mr. Frank trying to hold on to Robert's arm. Robert was squirming in every direction.

"LET HIM GO!" yelled Sam.

Sam grabbed Robert's arm and tried to pull him away from Mr. Frank.

"HELP!" yelled Robert.

"LET HIM GO YOU MONSTER-MAKER," shrieked Sam . . . and he pulled Robert so hard that suddenly Mr. Frank lost his grip for a second and Robert was free.

"RUN!" cried Sam.

Mr. Frank was standing in front of the elevator.

Sam pushed open the door to the stairwell and half shoved Robert through. They started up.

They heard the door to the stairwell open behind them.

They ran as fast as they could, but they heard Mr. Frank's footsteps right beneath them. By the time they got to the ninth floor, they could hear Mr. Frank gasping for breath, but he didn't give up.

Sam and Robert were out of breath, too. They wanted to stop and rest, but they knew he'd catch them if they did, so they kept run-

ning up and up, but he was right behind them.

Finally they reached the nineteenth floor. They ran to their apartment and slammed the door behind them.

Just seconds later, they heard pounding on the door.

Mrs. Bamford hurried into the living room.

The pounding got louder.

"Where have you been?" she demanded. "It's seven o'clock in the morning!!" She peered through the peephole and saw Mr. Frank looking very angry.

"Don't let him in . . ." Sam warned.

Mr. Frank started to ring the doorbell while continuing to pound the door with his fist.

"Sam! Robert! What is happening?" asked Mrs. Bamford.

Sam and Robert were too scared and out of breath to talk.

Mrs. Bamford looked at them strangely, then she put the chain on the door and opened it a few inches.

"What do you want?" she asked.

Mr. Frank tried to talk, but he was breathing so hard from running up nineteen floors that he couldn't answer. He just gasped for breath.

"Are you all right?" asked Mrs. Bamford.

Mr. Frank shook his head. "No," he gasped.

"Your kids . . ." wheezed Mr. Frank. He couldn't continue.

Mrs. Bamford told Sam to go into the kitchen and get a glass of water. She unlocked the chain and handed Mr. Frank the glass, but she kept the door half closed.

"Now what is this all about?" she asked.

"Your kids have been fooling around in my storage room," said Mr. Frank. He gulped the water.

"It was . . . was . . . an . . . accident . . ." stammered Robert, nearly in tears.

"We broke . . . one of Frankenstein's . . . I mean, Mr. Frank's boxes," admitted Sam, turning a deep red.

"You had no business being in there," said Mrs. Bamford sternly. She turned to Mr. Frank. "Did they break anything valuable? Of course, we'll pay for it. . . ."

"Well . . ." said Mr. Frank. "It *was* only a box of burned-out tubes. *But* it's the principle. I don't like *anybody* touching my things."

"You're right," said Mrs. Bamford. "Sam, Robert, you owe Mr. Frank an apology and I want you to promise you won't go near his storage room again."

"We're sorry," said Sam. Robert's voice was barely above a whisper.

"Robert, speak up," said Mrs. Bamford.

"I'm sorry," said Robert, his eyes never leaving the ground. "I'll never do it again."

"I knew I'd catch you," said Mr. Frank with a curious smile on his lips. "I rigged up a walkie-talkie."

Mrs. Bamford looked astonished.

"You went to all that trouble to catch two little kids?" she asked.

"Yes, I've always been good with electricity," said Mr. Frank. "You might say it's my hobby." He handed Mrs. Bamford the empty glass, turned his back on her, and rang for the elevator.

"Keep your kids out of my way," he warned as the elevator doors opened.

"He is a very strange man," said Mrs. Bamford as she watched the elevator doors close. "Now, boys, I want to know what you were doing in his storage room."

Neither Sam nor Robert wanted to answer. Finally, Robert said, "Mr. Frank has enough wire in his basement to make a dozen monsters."

"You didn't think Mr. Frank was Frankenstein, did you?" asked Mrs. Bamford.

Robert nodded his head yes.

"Frankenstein isn't a real person," said Mrs.

Bamford. "I think you and Sam were only scaring yourselves."

Sam and Robert just looked at each other.

A week later, coming home from school, Sam and Robert discovered a moving van in front of their apartment house. Mr. Clem and Mr. Christiansen sat on a bench watching the moving men go back and forth carrying heavy boxes. Each box had "Frank" written on it.

"Is Mr. Frank moving out?" Sam asked Mr. Clem.

"Thank goodness, yes," said Mr. Clem. "I had to complain to the landlord almost a dozen times about the noises that came out of that man's apartment. They were awful."

"He said there were too many people meddling in his business," said Mr. Christiansen.

"Ha!" said Mr. Clem. "He called himself a composer. I don't call that music. I'm going to throw away my earplugs."

"Is he gone?" asked Robert.

"Yup," said Mr. Christiansen. "There go the last of his boxes now." The moving men closed up the back of the truck and drove off.

Sam and Robert went down to the basement and over to Mr. Frank's storage room. The door was open. The room was empty. All the wires and boxes were gone. They walked in and looked around.

"I'm glad he's gone," said Robert.

"Me too," said Sam. He started to wander around the tiny room. Robert followed him. Suddenly Robert stepped on something. It felt both soft and crunchy.

"Yuk!" said Robert, jumping away from whatever he had stepped on.

"What's wrong?" asked Sam.

Robert bent down to see what he had stepped on. It was his Dracula doll, covered with dust. He picked it up and shook out Dracula's cape.

"Look!" said Robert, pointing to Dracula's shoulder. The arm had been ripped off.

"How weird," said Sam.

"Somebody pulled his arm off," said Robert.

"It must have been Frankenstein," whispered Sam.

"But why would he do that?" asked Robert.

"Well, Frankenstein needs arms and legs to make his monster . . ." Sam said slowly.

"Sam . . . you didn't think he really was Frankenstein . . . did you?" asked Robert.

"I wonder where he's going," said Sam. "He must be moving into another apartment house."

Don't miss these other monster books starring Sam and Robert Bamford written by Elizabeth Levy

Published by Harper Trophy Paperback Books

Dracula Is a Pain in the Neck

by Elizabeth Levy
illustrated by
Mordicai Gerstein

Robert thought that bringing his Dracula doll to Camp Hunter Creek was a good idea. Now he wishes he hadn't done it. All of the campers are calling him a vampire, and Robert is afraid their teasing is making the *real* Dracula angry. Frightening things have been happening around the camp. Unearthly howling noises have been heard after sundown. And one night, Sam and Robert see something that chills their very bones . . . .

Is Dracula haunting Camp Hunter Creek? And if he is, will Robert be his next victim?

Gorgonzola Zombies in the Park

by Elizabeth Levy
illustrated by
George Ulrich

When their awful cousin Mabel comes to visit, Sam and Robert decide to give her a scare. They make up a story about a voodoo zombie with breath as stinky as Gorgonzola cheese, who haunts Central Park and turns living things to statues.

At first Robert thinks the stories are funny. But lately he's noticed creepy things are happening in the park. Like the strange footprints—not human, not animal—that appear on the ground one day.

Now both Sam and Robert are worried. The Gorgonzola Zombie is just something they made up . . . isn't it?